&

volume 1

# THE MUSIC OF EVERYTHING

written & illustrated by Alexis Cohen
design by Brent Bishop


starbellypublishing.com
ISBN 978-0-9912673-0-9

 Published 2013. Printed in the United States of America

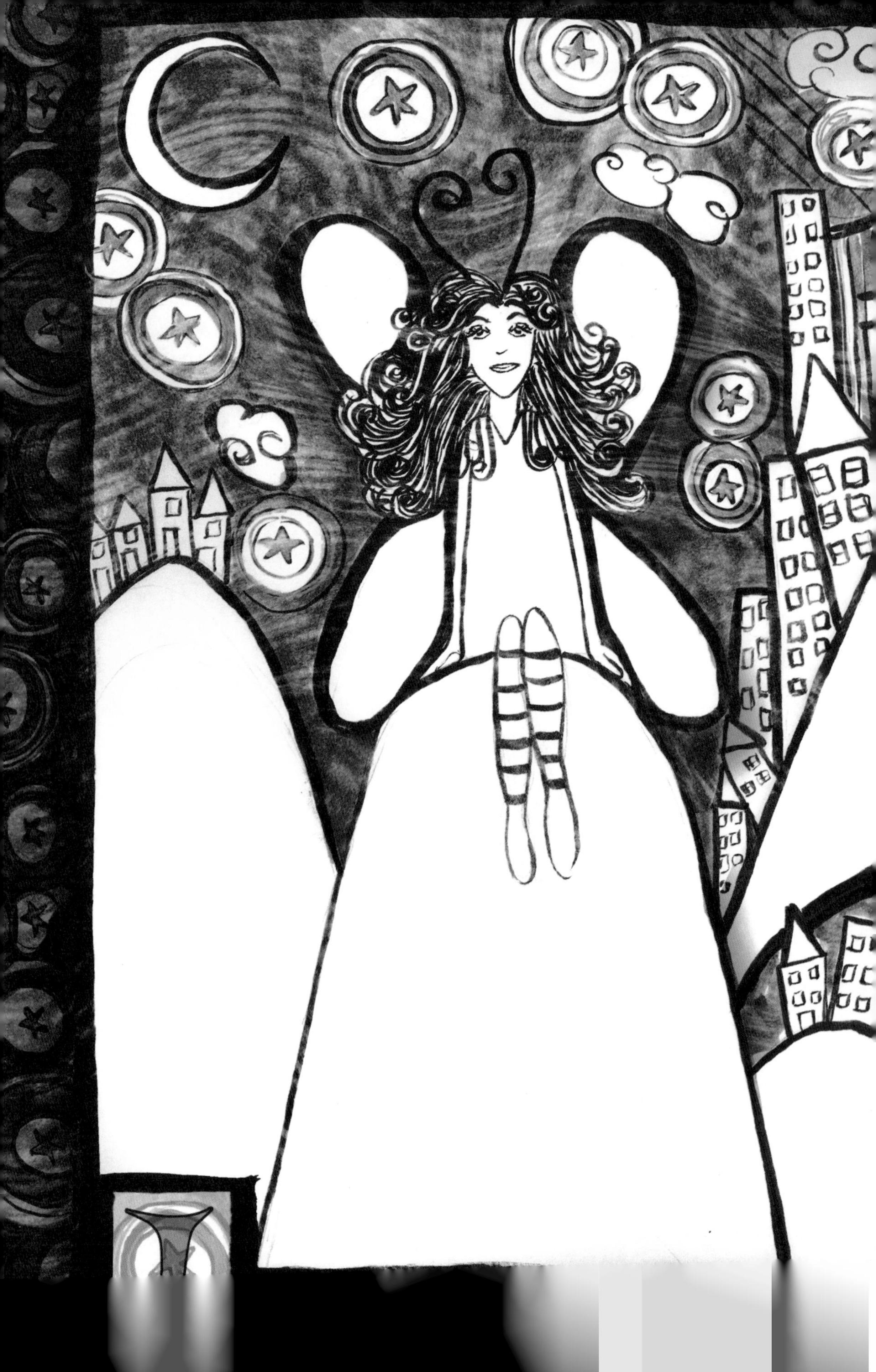

Waiting for day
to turn into night

The world comes alive - is ready to play
the music of everything swirls and it sways

Its magic whisper catches my hair
sweet smelling perfume floats in the air

I dance with the sea
I sing with the moon

LA LA LA
LA
LA LA LA

I dance and I dance
among stars in the sky

Bouncing and playing
I tumble and fly

The sky looks on

and claps with glee

A single star falls

and is given to me

"What is this?" I ask. "Your gift," she replies

This will help you in the darkest of skies

You hear the world's music
as it pulses with joy

I will teach you to use it
much more than a toy

Your quest must begin
not a moment too late

You may look back
but do not wait

When no tune is heard
when nothing sounds nice

I beg you to listen
to hear my advice

Feeling uncertain
not sure where you are

Monsters may scare you -
Remember Your Star!

Listen so closely
there's nothing to fear

The monsters will fade
your path becomes clear

R ide in its waves
in water and land

THIS WAY
YOU ARE ALMOST THERE
THIS WAY...
THIS WAY

How do I get up there?
YOU HAVE WINGS
REMEMBER YOU CAN FLY!!

"I did it, I did it!" you sing with delight,
"I found my way out, I moved through the night!"

Thank You!
SQUEEZE
HUG
SQUEEZE
SQUEEZE
HUG
Hold your star closely, it glows in your heart
it stays there forever, you never will part

You will shine brighter, led by your spark
helping guide others lost in the dark

## About the Author

Alexis Cohen lives with her sweetie Brent Bishop in San Francisco, where they dream on paper with words & art.

9922120R00020

Made in the USA
San Bernardino, CA
01 April 2014

JAYA
the nighttime faerie
&
volume 1
THE MUSIC OF EVERYTHING
written & illustrated by Alexis Cohen
design by Brent Bishop